E
HOB

Hobbie, Holly.

Toot & Puddle.

$15.95   02/02/2009

Toot & Puddle
Take a Leap!

Based on the teleplay by Stu Krieger
Adapted by Laura F. Marsh

NATIONAL GEOGRAPHIC
Washington, D.C.

For Holly and Doug
— L.F.M.

Founded in 1888, the National Geographic Society is one of the largest nonprofit scientific and educational organizations
in the world. It reaches more than 285 million people worldwide each month through its official journal, NATIONAL GEOGRAPHIC,
and its four other magazines; the National Geographic Channel; television documentaries; radio programs; films; books;
videos and DVDs; maps; and interactive media. National Geographic has funded more than 8,000 scientific research projects
and supports an education program combating geographic illiteracy.

For more information, please call
1-800-NGS-LINE (647-5463) or write to the following address:
NATIONAL GEOGRAPHIC SOCIETY
1145 17th Street N.W., Washington, D.C. 20036-4688 U.S.A.

Visit us online at www.nationalgeographic.com/books
Librarians and teachers, visit us at www.ngchildrensbooks.org
Visit Toot and Puddle online at www.nationalgeographic.com/tootandpuddle/

For more information about special discounts for bulk purchases, please contact
National Geographic Books Special Sales: ngspecsales@ngs.org.

For rights or permissions inquiries, please contact
National Geographic Books Subsidiary Rights: ngbookrights@ngs.org.

Library of Congress Cataloging-in-Publication Data available from the publisher on request.
Trade Paperback ISBN: 978-1-4263-0416-3
Reinforced Library Edition ISBN: 978-1-4263-0417-0

Printed in USA

One summer day, Toot and Puddle were painting their fence.

Toot took a break to watch Tulip making graceful circles in the air. "Doesn't flying look like fun?" he asked.

"Yup," Puddle agreed.

"You know, I've always wanted to skydive," said Toot. "Do you want to go together? We could sign up today!"

"Whoa, wait just a minute," Puddle said. "Skydiving sounds exciting, but I'm not sure I'm ready for that."

Toot was disappointed. "Why not?"

"Because . . . I'm afraid," Puddle said. "I get all shivery and quivery just thinking about it."

"Well, maybe I should try it first," said Toot, "and then I can tell you all about it when I land."

"Okay, but can I come along?" asked Puddle. "Just to watch," he added quickly.

"Absolutely," said Toot.

When they arrived at the lesson, Puddle explained to the instructor that he was just going to watch.

The first lesson was jumping practice.

Toot was having a wonderful time. "You should try it, Puds!"

Jumping did look like fun. Puddle decided to try.

"Look at me!" he said on his highest bounce.

Then it was time to practice
landing with a parachute.

"Keep your knees bent,"
called the instructor, "and if
you lose your balance, tuck
and roll."

Puddle wasn't sure he could
do this. Toot reassured him
that he could.

Toot and Puddle jumped
together, bent their knees,
and landed smoothly.

"Wow, that was great!"
exclaimed Toot.

"Thanks," said Puddle. "It
wasn't scary at all."

"So, will you come sky-
diving with me tomorrow?"
Toot asked.

His friend was quiet for
a moment. "I need to think
about it," Puddle said.

The next day, Toot and Puddle stood near the plane. The engine was running, and it was time to go.

"What do you think, Puds?" Toot asked. "This is your last chance. Are you coming?"

"Uh . . . no, thanks," Puddle replied. "I'm happy to watch. But thanks for the encouragement, Toot. I never knew what I could do until I tried."

As the plane rose higher and higher, Toot could see their house way down below. It looked teeny tiny.

Suddenly Toot wasn't sure that he could jump.

"I do want to," Toot said. "I'm just . . ."

"Scared?" the instructor asked. Toot nodded.

"Don't forget that you've practiced," said the instructor. "And I'll be right beside you."

Then Toot remembered what Puddle had told him: you never know what you can do until you try.

"I think I can do it!" exclaimed Toot.

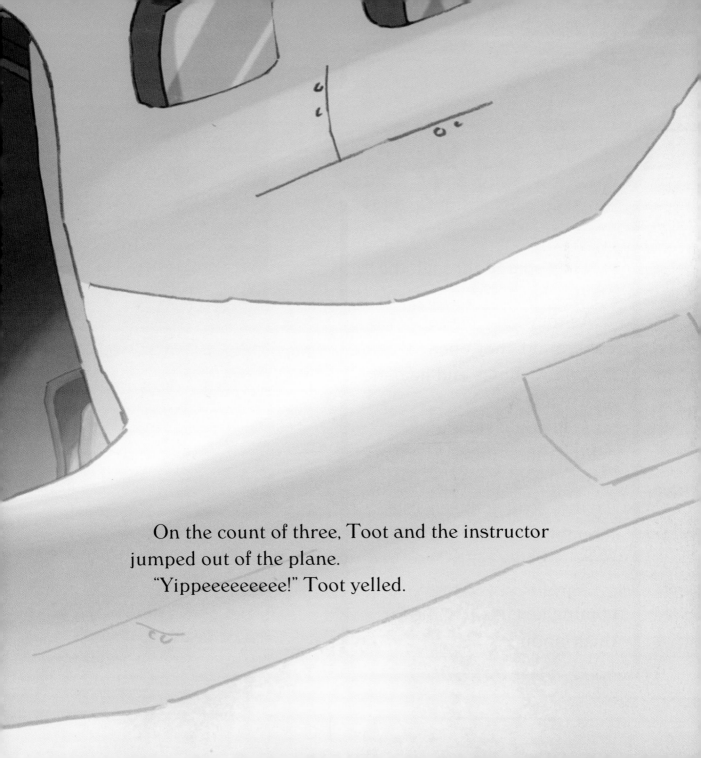

On the count of three, Toot and the instructor
jumped out of the plane.
"Yippeeeeeeeee!" Toot yelled.

They soared through the air like birds.

As they got closer to the ground, they opened their parachutes and floated slowly down.

Toot could see Puddle calling out to him.

It sounds like he's saying "send some cheese!" thought Toot. *But that doesn't make sense.*

Now the ground was coming fast. It was time for their landing.

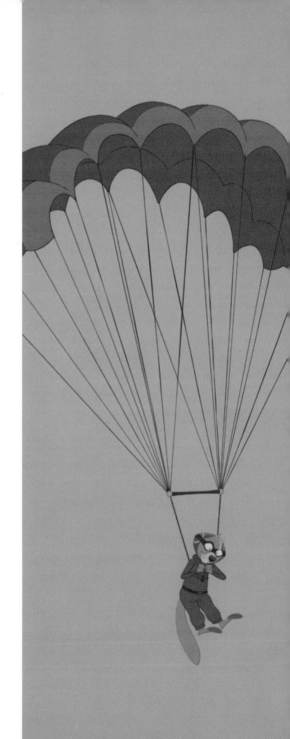

Toot bent his knees . . . and landed gracefully near Puddle.

"You did it! You did it!" Puddle cried, running over to his friend.

"That was fantastic!" said Toot. "But why were you telling me to 'send some cheese'?"

Puddle laughed and shook his head. "I was reminding you to 'bend your knees'!"

Back home in their garden, Puddle told Toot how cool it was to watch him skydive, but Toot was already thinking ahead. "What should our next adventure be?"

"A nice long nap sounds good to me," said Puddle with a smile.

"That's not an adventure!" Toot laughed.

"It is if you have a great dream," said Puddle.

"We could go spelunking!" Toot suggested. "That's what you do when you explore caves."

"Wouldn't it be dark down there?" Puddle asked with a shiver.

"Yup. And cool and exciting," Toot answered. "You know what I always say, Puds: The more places you go, the more you know!"